JEFI

Sangeeta Pandey is a senior journalist, writer and freelance editor. She is also a consultant (visiting faculty) at Amity University, where she teaches mass communication. She lives in Lucknow with her family and dogs. She likes to travel, listen to music and read. Once in a while, she likes to get away from the city's hustle and bustle and spend time at her farm, surrounded by nature.

THE MAKING OF THE GREATEST
JEFF BEZOS

Sangeeta Pandey

Editor: Payal Kumar

RUPA

Published by
Rupa Publications India Pvt. Ltd 2019
7/16, Ansari Road, Daryaganj
New Delhi 110002

Sales Centres:
Allahabad Bengaluru Chennai
Hyderabad Jaipur Kathmandu
Kolkata Mumbai

ISBN: 978-93-5333-642-4

First impression 2019

10 9 8 7 6 5 4 3 2 1

The moral right of the author has been asserted.

Printed at Nutech Print Services, Faridabad

CONTENTS

NOTE FROM THE EDITOR

Many new businesses come up every year globally, but only a small fraction of these succeed. And from among these, there rises only one Jack Ma, or Bill Gates, or Mark Zuckerberg, or Jeff Bezos. What are the factors that catapult these entrepreneurs to success?

Discover the true stories of the world's greatest entrepreneurs. These are extraordinary men who challenged conventional wisdom about money and great formal education being the prerequisites for success. What are those qualities that enabled them to create success out of adversity? What inspired them to have the courage to believe in their ideas, to dream big when resources were minimal, and to persevere when things seemed to go wrong? This series explores how these entrepreneurs, who became common household names, not only scripted exemplary success for themselves, but also changed the world forever.

Dr Payal Kumar

THE MAN

As the hot June wind whispered through the by-lanes of the oldest city in the world — Kashi — locals sought solace in the cool nooks and corners of old buildings, sipping a kulhad of lassi or drinking water from the small pouches sold by street urchins everywhere.

Many foreign tourists, meanwhile, preferred to beat the heat either by sitting in the shade of trees, temples and old buildings near the iconic ghats of the Ganga or by simply sharing a chillum with the babas — Shiv bhakts — dotting the city.

For a curious few foreigners, walking in the shade of buildings, exploring the myriad stalls selling delicious street food — from baati chokha to kachori and jalebis — seemed like an experience of a lifetime.

As the scorching sun started its downward descent, the humidity became unbearable. People thronged the ghats for a boat ride on the mighty Ganga to beat the heat. The majestic ghats where the different stages of life can be observed in all their glory, as seen from a boat on the river, is a view that draws millions from all over the world. It was no different for the world's first centi-billionaire Jeff Bezos, founder of the largest online global retailer, Amazon. Clad in a cotton shirt, trousers and loafers, Bezos, along with his former wife and children, on their maiden trip to Kashi in June 2018, keenly observed the unique display along the Ganga. As their boat, decorated with flowers, stopped near the Manikarnika ghat, where cremations take place all day long, Bezos was fascinated by the final ritual in the life of a Hindu.

When the boat started moving, Bezos looked back towards the burning pyres once again and then motioned to the captain to stop at another ghat where he got off. Even as his family stayed on board, Bezos made his way through the narrow by-lanes, stopping and inquiring about the local street food and how it was prepared. Language did not seem to be a barrier, as he communicated with the local vendors using gestures and signs, keenly observing their responses. 'I love interacting with people and learning things from them,' he had once said during an informal conversation with his brother at a talk show.

Cut to a few months back, when Bezos went aboard an open mini bus in Bengaluru. Clad in a white coat and trousers with a colourful bandhani scarf wrapped around his neck, he happily held the placard of his company on a promotion spree. This man, who could hire anyone in the world to promote his brand, preferred to take it head on and do it himself. As the road show progressed, Jeff remained busy, discussing Amazon and its offers for customers, for it is 'they who pay the money and not the rivals,' as he had famously said during Amazon's fledgling days when his rivals had started undercutting Amazon.

THE MAN: HIS CHILDHOOD

'**W**ork hard, have fun, make history.'
This motto of Jeffrey Preston Bezos, or Jeff
Bezos, aptly sums up his philosophy and
journey so far as the founder of Amazon. He believes
that life is all about taking risks and being resourceful—a
lesson he learned from his grandfather. And it was this
ability that made him the world's wealthiest person
when his net worth touched the $150 billion mark in
July 2018, according to *Forbes* magazine.

Bezos's first tryst with computers was in fourth
grade when he was living in Houston. There was a
teletype machine in his school that was connected to a
mainframe computer. A local businessman had donated
computer time to the students. Jeff would stay back

after school, along with two other children, and together they figured out the basics of programming. It was his love for computers and the Internet, and the fact that he 'did not want to regret not taking a chance' in his sunset years, that led him to Amazon.

Jeff Bezos was born on 12 January 1964 in Albuquerque, New Mexico. His mother Jacklyn Gise Jorgensen, a teenager at the time, and father Ted Jorgensen, 18, named their son Jeffrey Preston Jorgensen. The childhood of the future Amazon CEO was far from perfect. Ted was a circus performer and had problems with alcohol, which meant that he could not hold a job for very long. This ultimately frustrated Jacklyn so much that she decided to split from him. Within a year of their marriage, Jacklyn divorced Ted and asked him to stay away from their son.

During an interview on German television, Bezos recalled the difficulties faced by his mother as a single parent. 'Being pregnant at 17 years, when my mom was in high school, was not cool at all,' he recalled.

But Jacklyn never gave up. In April 1968, she married a Cuban immigrant, Miguel 'Mike' Bezos who adopted the four-year-old Jeff, whose surname was then changed to Bezos. After earning a degree from the

University of New Mexico, Mike and his family shifted to Houston, where he worked as an engineer for Exxon.

The subject of Bezos's parentage came up quite innocuously when he was six years old. The little boy had been playing with a friend and proudly told him that he had attended his parents' wedding. The friend had looked at him incredulously and said that was not possible since Jeff could not have been born at that time!

Surprised and confused, little Jeff went home and told his mother about the conversation. Jacklyn realized that the time had come to talk to Jeff about his parentage. She explained that she had been married earlier, but when that did not work out, she took him and went to live with her parents. The boy understood and simply asked his mother whether she had got a divorce, to which she nodded in affirmative.

Many years later, Bezos acknowledged his mother's sacrifices in a tweet, 'I won the lottery with my mom. Thanks for literally everything, Mom.'

'From the minute I knew Jeff was going to be born, all I wanted to do was be a good mother,' recalls Jacklyn. She took her son to her community college classes, where she tended to his needs during lunchtime. When little Jeff was two, Jacklyn started working at a bank, where she met her future husband Mike, who later confessed that he fell in love with both mother and son simultaneously.

For Bezos, Mike is his *father*, and the only time he ever thinks about his biological father (Ted) is when he has to fill up medical forms.

Jacklyn and Mike had two other children—Mark and Christina—with whom Bezos bonded very well.

Incidentally, Bezos's pet name is 'Tim'.

On a talk show, Bezos recounted that his stepfather Mike is Mexican and speaks the language, where the alphabet 'J' is silent. Now, the irony is that both his wife and son's names begin with 'J' and as a result, Mike goes around calling them 'eff' and 'ackyln', and the entire family laughs about it even today!

Young Bezos wasn't much of a sports lover. He loved the world of books and experimentation. The love of academics, especially science and mathematics, got him to read most of the books on these subjects in the school library. He also loved carrying out experiments, even on classmates. It was no surprise that he was among the toppers in his class, much to the relief of his mother. In fact, he even helped coach his siblings.

His ingenuity can be gauged from the fact he

designed a survey to rate the sixth grade teachers at his school. The objective was to carry out a statistical analysis for the mathematics class with the help of his survey. The survey was designed to evaluate instructors' ability to teach. Fellow students were asked to fill up the survey forms, after which young Jeff drew up a statistical analysis of the teachers' performance.

However, according to his teachers, he did not possess strong leadership skills.

Bezos also had a competitive streak, even in his early years. One of his classmates was a voracious reader who claimed to read twelve books a week, and young Jeff would try to keep up with her. This is no surprise, as he is a book lover even now.

However, the man who inspired him to delve deep into things and have an inquisitive mind was his grandfather. Lawrence Preston Gise, who was the regional director of the US Atomic Energy Commission (AEC) in Albuquerque, was Bezos's maternal grandfather.

Gise retired early to live in his family's ranch near Cotulla, Texas, where Bezos spent a major part of his childhood. The children fondly called Gise 'Pop'. Bezos's maternal grandmother was Mattie Louise Gise, and he is also a cousin of country singer George Strait.

The children spent a lot of time with their grandparents, especially Pop, at his ranch, between the ages of four and sixteen. While recalling his days at the ranch, Bezos said he learned everything there, from repairing a generator and fixing windmills to treating animals and even laying pipelines.

The sprawling ranch with a barn, homestead, shed and cattle, proved to be an ideal place for the children to experiment and learn. They would do all the work on the farm, including 'castrating bulls' as Bezos jokingly said years later. From helping Pop lay pipelines to repairing the barn, they did it all. Bezos and Pop even built a house from a professional kit. The specialists had laid the foundation, after which everything was done by grandfather and grandson.

The brothers also recalled the time they had overhauled a bulldozer that Pop had bought for $5000. 'Pop purchased it at a throwaway price because it was completely broke. The gears wouldn't work, the engine was totally conked,' Bezos recounted in an interview. On seeing its condition, Pop first had to get a crane to lift the engine, as it was too heavy to be lifted manually. Thereafter, they started dismantling the whole thing. One by one, as the pieces came out, Pop would explain their uses to his grandchildren. Then began the arduous task of repairing the defunct parts, which was a challenge as most of them were beyond their working life.

However, without calling for any help, Pop would start repairing them, learning by trial and error. Jeff and Mark would pass on the tools to him and watch him keenly as he went about the Herculean task. Every day after finishing the early morning work at the ranch, the trio would head to the yard shed to repair the machine. Slowly, piece by piece, the entire thing started falling into place. Finally, when the entire bulldozer was reassembled, Pop asked them to fetch gasoline to start the contraption. As the bulldozer came to life, Pop smiled while the boys jumped with joy. This project had taken them an entire summer, and finally seeing it come to life was the best thing they could have wished for.

They celebrated the occasion with a special dinner as Pop rewarded them with a memento for their efforts. Jeff and Mark could not stop grinning, as Pop was a man of few words and his acknowledgement was a big thing for the children.

'My grandfather was a very resourceful man.

While my mother and (step)father influenced me, but it was my grandfather who left a lasting impression. Whenever there would be a problem, grandpa would not call for any help, rather he would try and fix it himself. I learned to be resourceful from him and, as an individual, learned to rely on myself. Later, when I founded the company (Amazon), it was this attitude and team resourcefulness that helped us to become what we are today,' said Bezos.

Another thing that Pop was fond of doing, was fixing windows and the children would follow him. Right from repairing a roof to fixing barns they did it all. Pop's resourcefulness can be gauged from the fact that he even made the needles with which he would suture farm cattle. 'Can you imagine someone making a needle?' Bezos asked the audience at a talk show and beamed proudly as he said, 'Pop did it.'

The children remember Pop taking a piece of metal and blow-torching it, after which he would flatten it by hammering, to resemble a needle, following which he would then make a hole. 'It was incredulous. He was so self-reliant and resourceful,' remarked the brothers at a talk show.

However, the most important lesson Bezos learned

from his grandfather came after he wisecracked to his grandmother about the many minutes of her life she had lost while smoking in the car. The incident took place when Jeff was going somewhere with his grandparents, in a car. A chain smoker, his grandmother was going about her business as a commercial on the hazards of smoking was playing on the radio. The narrator rattled off statistics about the minutes of life reduced by smoking just one cigarette.

Young Jeff quickly calculated the number of cigarettes his grandmother smoked during the car ride and told her the minutes of life she had lost. On hearing this, she burst into tears at which point his grandfather stopped the car and stepped outside asking him to follow suit. Taken aback, the young boy looked at Pop who told him, 'You're going to figure out one day that it's harder to be kind than clever.'

The boy never forgot.

Staying at Pop's ranch was one of the highlights for Jeff and his siblings. Lying on a carpet watching television as Neil Armstrong stepped on the moon or listening to news bulletins on the infamous 'Watergate scandal', which was zealously followed by Pop, was the genesis of his ambitious space travel venture Blue

Origin and, of course, the ownership of the iconic newspaper *The Post*, as admitted by him during various interviews.

Stepbrother Mark recalled how fascinated Bezos was with space travel and would keenly follow the *Star Trek* series and anything to do with 'the final frontier'. In addition, Pop, who had already worked at the space centre, would tell him fascinating stories about the distant world. Lying in his room, he would often dream of exploring the 'final frontier'.

Even Bezos's graduation speech was all about space travel. Space was his first love but computer and Internet were not very far behind.

Unlike Bezos, Mark has an entirely different outlook in life. He is also the more muscular of the two. Mark is in charge of development for a non-profit organization called Robinhood. He also pitches in for a poverty-fighting charity in New York and as a voluntary firefighter. The brothers believe in the philosophy, 'Not every day is going to offer us a chance to save somebody's life, but every day offers us an opportunity to affect one,' that Mark revealed during a series of TED talks in California.

Mark is president of the Scarsdale Schools Education

Foundation, which raises money to help supplement the Scarsdale School District budget. The group has helped fund Maker Spaces at five Scarsdale elementary schools, which allow students to design, prototype and work with 3D printers. The foundation is also raising money to construct a design lab at Scarsdale High School. Mark has four children. His two daughters attend high school, while the sons study at private elementary schools. Mark appears occasionally in the biographies and interviews of his elder brother, but overall, he prefers to keep a low profile.

Not much is known about Bezos's stepsister Christina, but being the youngest, she got all the attention from her brothers. Christina had a horse called Red that she would ride on the ranch, as her brothers kept an eye on her lest she fall. Bezos credits his parents for the close bond shared by the three siblings. Mark was born when Bezos was just under 10 years old, and Christina was born soon after. The fraternal feelings for his siblings soon turned into friendship. Even then, Bezos kept his siblings on their toes by devising new experiments to keep them out of his room when they would barge in. Both Mark and Christina would then devise ways to get in anyway.

Today, even as they have their own families, once a year, the siblings, along with their spouses, go on an annual trip without the children who are left in the care of Jacklyn. Jeff says it was his mother's idea and now they happily follow it. Incidentally, the Bezos siblings have eleven children between themselves, and as Mark quipped in a talk show, 'We are making sure that the world population doesn't go down.'

MARRIAGE AND CHILDREN

'I want to marry someone who can get me out of a
third world prison,' the Amazon honcho famously
told this to his friends when they asked him about
the kind of life partner he wanted, before setting him
up on blind dates. He was looking for a 'resourceful'
person and the search for this ideal partner led him on
endless blind dates, so much so that he once jokingly
admitted to have become a 'professional blind dater'.

After endless cups of coffee on innumerable blind
dates, he had almost given up on finding his ideal
partner. 'I would meet these girls and after sometime,
we wouldn't have anything common to talk about.
Finally, we would exchange tips on how to tackle the
next blind date,' he told the audience at a talk show

with his brother.

The hairline had started receding by then, and he was busy with his job at DE Shaw in Manhattan, where he was working as an investment banker. It was here that he first met Mackenzie Tuttle, a research associate at the firm. She was a Californian, her father was working as a financial planner and mother was a homemaker. She had attended the Hotchkiss School in Connecticut and graduated from the Princeton University.

It was attraction at first sight for Bezos and Mackenzie. An athletic brunette, Mackenzie had a charming smile and sharp eyes that saw everything. Bezos too was in the same league in terms of his looks, albeit with a receding hairline.

However, it wasn't her appearance that caught his attention. It was her credentials as a professional that impressed him the most. 'I was lucky to see her CV first, before I met her. I knew she was resourceful and later, when I met her...the rest is history,' Bezos told Mathias Dopfner in an interview.

The duo worked together for several hours daily and Bezos became increasingly more infatuated with her. He finally seemed to have found someone who was funny, resourceful and, most importantly, made him laugh. Conversations between them were never boring, instead they liked spending time together.

Despite the attraction, Bezos was scared of asking Mackenzie out, because he was apprehensive about being charged with harassment. He would watch her from the corner of his eyes, spend hours on projects with her, but as soon as office hours were up, they would go their separate ways. Mackenzie also admitted later in an interview that she was attracted to Bezos and his pleasant demeanour very pleasing, and thought their conversations were very intellectual but, at the same time, natural.

After observing him closely, Mackenzie finally broke the ice and asked Bezos out to lunch. This proved to be a turning point in their relationship. Professional bonhomie and mutual attraction gave way to a full-fledged courtship. Their instinctive comfort and camaraderie resulted in a whirlwind romance. When Bezos introduced Mackenzie to his parents within a few months of dating, they took to her instantly. Jacklyn was happy for her son, as was Mike, for they found Mackenzie to be a level-headed woman who was ideal for Bezos.

Within three months of their first lunch date, the

duo got engaged and tied the knot in 1992, within six months of their meeting.

The couple's contrasting personalities form a perfect foil for each other. While Bezos is a gregarious person, Mackenzie prefers the comfort of home and family. 'He likes to meet people. He's a very social guy. Cocktail parties for me can be nerve-wracking. The brevity of conversations, the number of them—it's not my sweet spot,' she once told a fashion magazine. Together, they were one of the most powerful couples in the business world.

In her spare time, Mackenzie likes to write. Fond of literature, Mackenzie also participated in a writing course under the guidance of writer Toni Morrison, who called her one of the best writers in the class. She won the 2006 American Book Award. Some of her famous books are *Traps* and *The Testing of Luther Albright*.

The Testing of Luther Albright was lauded by critics and narrates the story of Luther Albright, a designer of dams, a self-controlled man who believes he can make his family happy by sheltering them from his own emotions, till an earthquake shakes the very foundation of his life. It is the story of an ordinary man who is tested and strives to do everything to shelter his family and bring everything under control.

In the initial days, Mackenzie would ask Bezos to go through her manuscripts. The day she told him her manuscript was ready, Bezos would leave everything at office and make a beeline for home, to read her work. Even when she told him that it could wait, he did not listen, so Mackenzie adopted another approach. She decided that she would tell him about a manuscript only when he was home and had a weekend to spare.

His suggestions, if feasible, were incorporated into the manuscript. According to Bezos, Mackenzie is happiest while pursuing her literary career, which she took a break from when her husband started his company.

Even when the family expanded, Mackenzie continued with her literary pursuits, something she feels is important for her to maintain her individuality and also continue honing her writing skills.

Today the couple has four children — three sons and a daughter. The eldest son, Prezton was born in 2000, followed by two more sons. Later, they adopted a girl from China, who is the youngest of the lot.

FAMILY MAN

'I have hit the jackpot with my mother and family.' The couple has a very hands-on parenting approach and Bezos credits Mackenzie for this. In fact, Mackenzie got some basic tools that are out of bounds for other children and let the trio experiment with them. 'She prefers a resourceful child with nine fingers instead of a non-resourceful kid with all fingers intact,' Bezos remarked jokingly during a chat show. The children, like their parents when they were young, are encouraged to do things on their own and learn to be resourceful.

To ensure overall development of their children, the couple takes them travelling during off-season, to kitchen-science experiments and Mandarin lessons, and involve them with local clubs and sporting activities with their neighbour's children. Travelling seems to be the favourite pastime of the Bezos family. Mackenzie does most of the planning, keeping in mind her husband's passion for his work and the children's holidays. Short, fun-filled trips that also incorporate educational learning for the children, are her favourite.

The family time that Bezos had growing up, is there even today. He prefers to have breakfast with his wife and children, so he never schedules any early morning meetings. Till a few years ago, Mackenzie even dropped Bezos to the office. 'The Bezos are such a normal, close-knit family, it's almost abnormal,' said family friend Danny Hillis, when asked by a magazine reporter.

Mackenzie's love for Bezos is apparent when she fondly says that watching her husband build Amazon was the most amazing thing for her. 'To me, watching your spouse, somebody that you love, have an adventure, what is better than that?' she said.

Besides business, her husband's penchant for experimenting with food is well known. Jeff Bezos has an unusual palate. During a meeting with Woot founder Matt Rutledge, he ordered octopus along with other breakfast staples like eggs, bacon, bread, etc. 'I must have the breakfast octopus,' he told Rutledge. And there's more, the man is particularly fond of roasted iguana!

Recalling a piece of trivia about his eating habits, Bezos once said that in his teens and even after he got married, he would eat anything that would taste good. The Amazon honcho's breakfast during his college and Wall Street days was a whole can of Pillsbury biscuits. 'I would get up in the morning and preheat the oven to 375 degrees; empty a can of Pillsbury biscuit on a baking tray lined with baking sheet and put butter on it. After a few minutes when it was done, I would have my breakfast and go out,' recalls Bezos with his trademark laugh.

He never put on weight.

Post marriage, the ritual continued and after watching it for three months, Mackenzie finally asked him one day, 'Do you know what's in that (biscuit)?' Bezos was clueless as he had never read a nutrition label till then and ate what tasted good. Afterwards, Mackenzie had a 'rudimentary' discussion about nutrition with her husband.

He is also not averse to trying vegetarian food, even the sattvik kind without onion and garlic, as he did during his visit to Kashi. He seemed to enjoy the delicacies that Kashi had to offer.

Another thing that Bezos loves is to make cocktails. His fantasy job is to be a bartender someday, Bezos confessed at a talk show. Mark swears by his brother's cocktail-making skills. 'I can rustle up a pretty good cocktail as I love making them. However, the process is time-consuming,' admits Bezos and jokes that there would be a signboard behind his bar that would read: 'You can either have it (cocktail) good or fast.' He is the family's favourite go-to man for cocktails during special gatherings and even on weekends.

After a good round of drinks, food and conversation, Bezos loves to snooze. However, here is the difference: unlike many achievers who sleep for just four to five hours, he is a firm believer in shut-eye, even on regular days. He sleeps for about eight hours every day and gets up early morning without an alarm clock! He said it helps him to continuously make good decisions. The shut-eye also saves him from 'decision fatigue'. 'Eight hours of sleep makes a big difference for me, and I try hard to make that a priority,' Bezos said in an interview with *Thrive Global*.

Sometimes he also brings a sleeping bag to work

in an attempt to recharge himself on difficult days. He reasons it out with simple logic. 'Senior executives have to make three to four quality decisions for a fat paycheque. And if they are tired, it doesn't help,' he said during an interview with David Rubenstein. A full eight hours of sleep ensures that a person is not tired 'or stressed out, and can logically make those quality decisions that would have a major impact on a company.

Who is going to question this logic when the man is laughing all the way to the bank!

A firm believer of going on holidays, the entrepreneur also makes it a point to have family vacations. He has been spotted with the entire family, vacationing across the globe, including with parents Mike and Jacklyn. The trips help to not only rejuvenate, but also forge a stronger bond between the siblings, their spouses and parents. In fact, many quirky pictures of Bezos posing with Mackenzie outside famous local eateries or even lifting her up at famous tourist sites often make their way to the couple's fridge door. Goofing around is something they enjoy to the hilt.

During a talk show with Mark, the Amazon honcho shared memories of the trips they had together, lasting from five days to thirty days. During one such adventure trip to Texas, the siblings, along with Christina's husband, had gone camping and mountaineering. They drove cross-country, explored caves and went rock-climbing. Another one was about camping and horse riding. 'We were on horseback for five days and by the end of it, my butt was sore,' Bezos recounted as he winked at Mark.

In fact, during family gatherings around a fire with bourbons, Bezos toasts with: 'To adventure and fellowship.' It is also something he repeats everyday at dinner with Mackenzie and the children. When questioned, Bezos replied that one had the choice to 'choose between a life of comfort or service and adventure.' He was sure that the one thing that anyone would regret not doing when they were 80 years old was 'not going for a life of service and adventure' and hence his toast.

Adventure for Jeff Bezos is also about doing something new that makes one happy and not live in 'stasis', while fellowship is about a journey with family and friends. This is something that he not only believes in, but also follows.

Recalling one such adventure, the Blue Origin

founder said that they had gone on a month-long expedition to the Atlantic to recover Apollo 11 engines that had been lying in the sea for four decades. The 300-foot hi-tech boat had every amenity and sixty crew, all men, on board with the exception of Jacklyn. 'My mother wanted to be a part of the expedition, so both Mark and I took her along. However, I had not anticipated what was coming next. As we boarded the ship, the captain, who was a Norwegian guy, came to me and sought my permission to remove all the porn stashed in the vessel as it was the first time a woman was coming on a mission that had mostly men. I laughed and well... we never found any objectionable material during the expedition,' Bezos laughed and said.

That signature laughter of Jeff Bezos is famous. As the man once told an interviewer, 'I am a good audience.' He loves to laugh out loud and remembers a time during his childhood years and even his teens when both Mark and Christina did not go to see films with him as he laughed out too loudly. The boycott continued for several years, says Bezos with another guffaw. Does it continue even today? He nods an emphatic 'No'.

Today, however, the laugh has become his trademark

and even under stress he prefers smiling or laughing. A colleague once asked him why and he quipped, 'I would be crying otherwise.'

In 2003, Bezos scraped past death when, during a scouting tour in Texas for the right piece of land to test Blue Origin rockets, his chopper crashed. The billionaire suffered minor injuries and recovered but the incident shook him to the core. 'Nothing extremely profound flashed through my head in those few seconds. My main thought was, this is such a silly way to die,' Bezos said in an interview in 2004. 'It wasn't life-changing in any major way. I've learned a fairly tactical lesson from it, I'm afraid. The biggest takeaway is: Avoid helicopters whenever possible! They're not as reliable as fixed-wing aircraft.'

This, in essence, is the man who wants to experience things firsthand while maintaining the work-life harmony that is so important to him. This philosophy, coupled with a wacky sense of humour, make him an inspiration for many.

THE EARLY YEARS AND EDUCATION

'[In business] what's dangerous is not to evolve.'

The foundations of Jeff Bezos's dreams were laid at his grandfather's sprawling ranch. That was not only a learning ground for him and his siblings, but also the home of some of his most cherished memories.

During a talk show with sibling Mark, the siblings recalled several such hilarious incidents that had a cascading effect on their lives. Incidentally, most of them related to Pop, who doted on them and would tell them stories about missile defence systems, besides teaching them many things.

Describing one such incident, the brothers said that after winding up the day's work outside the ranch, Pop would come home in his car and they would open the gate to let him in. One evening, the siblings were not at the gate and Pop thought he would slow down the car, get off and run to the gate which was situated downhill, and open it, after which he would get back into the car and then drive into the ranch. 'God only knows what Pop was thinking, but it backfired,' remembered Bezos with his customary laugh.

Pop followed his plan and reached the gate, but the car had picked up more speed than he had anticipated and before he could open the gate, it rammed into it, catching his thumb and severing a part. Instead of shouting in pain, Pop threw the severed bit into the bushes and called the children. He then drove all the way to a hospital situated some miles away.

When they reached the hospital, the doctor inspected the thumb and said that it could be joined with the missing part through surgery and asked for the severed bit. 'We looked at Pop, who told us that he had thrown it in the bushes,' said Mark. The family got in the car, which Pop drove again, and on reaching the ranch, young Jeff and his siblings started searching for the severed bit in the bushes where Pop indicated he had thrown it. However, it was not to be found. 'Probably some animal had eaten it by then,' the siblings laughingly recalled.

They went back to the hospital and told the doctor who did whatever he could to reconstruct the thumb. After some days, when the thumb had healed, the doctor said it would require skin grafting, which he said would be taken from Pop's butt. 'Pop agreed. The funny part is that after it healed completely, the part of thumb where the grafting was done, started growing butt hair, which Pop would shave everyday with his electric razor, after his beard. How we all laughed at it, but Pop just took it in his stride. It became a family legend that is shared even today when we gather for any occasion,' said Jeff.

The resilience and tenacity to take things as they come without breaking down, was something he learned from Pop, and it was one of the key lessons of his life. It helped him cope with losses even when Amazon became a name to be reckoned with and gave him the ability to continue experimenting and innovating.

Even as a child, Jeff was always dabbling with one experiment or another. He displayed scientific and technological prowess that literally kept the entire Bezos household on their toes. 'I would set up booby traps all over the house and at one point my parents were so scared that they would open a door and a whole bunch of nails would fall on them,' recalled the Amazon honcho during an interview.

The boy would even try these tricks on his siblings, Mark and Christina. He even rigged an electric alarm to keep them out of his room. He also built an infinity cube,' a toy on the lines of a kaleidoscope but with motorized mirrors. He would also dabble in robotics and other projects. Fed up with the clutter from his experiments, Jacklyn and Mike finally told their son to move his workshop to the garage.

Renamed 'Science Fair Central' by young Jeff, the garage became a lab for all his experiments. The catch, however, was getting parts and spares for technical experiments. It was here that Jacklyn came to the rescue. 'She would drive me to a radio shack to get the parts. Some days there would be multiple trips. Finally, my mother told me to make an inventory of all the things I needed as she would only make one trip to the shack daily,' said Bezos in an interview.

Support from the family and freedom to indulge in his scientific hobby played an important role in fuelling young Jeff's passion for computer and science. 'As a young boy, I'd been a garage inventor. I'd invented an automatic gate closer out of cement-filled tires, a solar cooker that didn't work very well out of an umbrella and tinfoil, baking-pan alarms to entrap my siblings,' he recounts. 'I'd always wanted to be an inventor, and she wanted me to follow my passion.'

That Jeff was a bright student was confirmed by a standardized test when he was eight years old. He was admitted into a pilot programme for gifted students at River Oaks Elementary School, Houston.

When he was nine years old, the book *Turning on Bright Minds: A Parent Looks at Gifted Education in Texas* described him as 'friendly but serious', a boy of 'general intellectual excellence'.

'It also said I had no leadership skills whatsoever,' he recalled years later with his trademark laughter.

Jeff's mother wanted him to go beyond books and so she signed him up for a youth football league. The boy, of course, was not at all happy about the scenario but he did what he even now does best—memorizing the team's offensive and defensive positions. The coach finally gave him the responsibility of calling plays on the field.

In 1978, Exxon transferred Miguel to Miami, where the family lived in a four-bedroom house with a pool in the affluent Palmetto district of Dade County. Jeff enrolled at Palmetto High, an incubator of high achievers. He also participated in the Student Science Training Program at the University of Florida and won a Silver Knight Award in 1982. At that time, Jeff, like most American students, worked at McDonald's as a line cook during breakfast hours. He gravitated to a group of about 10 children from his honours classes. They engaged in gentle hijinks, such as hanging yarn from classroom lights before school. 'He was not a problem kid,' says Jacklyn Bezos. 'If Jeff was ever guilty of anything, it was crimes of the mouth.'

After graduating from school, he left Miami for Princeton University, the only school he wanted to attend. 'Einstein was there, for goodness sake,' he said, and dreamed of becoming a theoretical physicist until he discovered that there were other students who were brighter than him in that field.

One night, Bezos was struggling with an equation and, after sometime, went to the dorm room of a classmate, who glanced at the equation and said, 'Cosine.' When Bezos expressed some doubts, the classmate went on to write three pages of equations to justify his answer.

The incident made Bezos realize that he was meant for other things, following which he switched his concentration to electrical engineering and computer science. And the rest, as they say, is history.

He graduated with a Bachelor of Science degree in electrical engineering, and a second one in computer science. In the university, he was also part of the honour societies Phi Beta Kappa and Tau Beta Pi. In addition, he was the president of the school's chapter of Students for the Exploration and Development of Space.

During college summer breaks, he would take up various jobs. In June 1984, he worked as a programmer/analyst in Norway, and the following year, he improved an IBM program in California.

All these experiences only whetted his appetite for technology. The chance to see a simple software programme, linking multitudes of computers or helping the virtual world, become a part of the real world and people only excited him further.

He was proud as a peacock about his technical skills and academic prowess. However, many years later, when asked about what he would like to change if given a chance to go back to university, he quipped, 'Be more confident about my decisions and actions rather than talent. 'When asked to elaborate, he said that at any given point an individual is born with special skillsets, but it is the decisions taken by them that make all the difference. 'What is important is to be confident about your beliefs and vision, following which you take a decision. Standing up for what you believe in is the difference between success and failure,' he said.

The writing was on the wall as the young man was ready to make history by being confident about his decision to start an e-commerce venture.

PROFESSIONAL JOURNEY

'One of the only ways to get out of a tight box is to invent your way out.'

It was the unconditional love of his parents, wife and grandparents that led an investment banker to become an entrepreneur. Both professional choices being poles apart, what made this youngster quit a lucrative job and take the risk was the fact that 'somebody had his back'.

'I think it is very important for an individual to know that they have some loving support for them to take a risk. It may not necessarily be starting a business venture. Risk can be anything that an individual wants to do to follow their passion. The courage to do so comes from unconditional support and the love of family and friends,' said the Amazon honcho in an interview.

Bezos was also passionate about his vision. During one of his lectures to students after Amazon's success, he told them, 'You guys will find that you have passion. Having a passion is a gift. I think we all have passion, but one has to be alert to it. If your passion is your calling, then you have hit the jackpot.'

After he graduated in 1986, Bezos turned down offers from several sought-after corporations like Intel, Bell Labs and Andersen Consulting among others, and instead took up a job at Fitel, a New York start-up, that was building a global telecommunications network to settle cross-border equity sales.

He liked the challenge and deemed the founders brilliant. He was their eleventh employee, entering the flamboyant domain of New York finance in the 1980s.

He slept on People Express planes and shuttled regularly across the Atlantic. At 24, he was head of customer service and software development, and those divisions were based in New York and London, respectively.

Fitel offered an early look at how connected computers could automate a business process. Bezos, adept at both debugging code and wooing clients, was part of a team that built what was essentially a mini-Internet for investors, sellers, brokers and banks.

But those clients tended to think conservatively about new technology, and Fitel struggled to attract new customers. In April 1988, Bezos left for a job at a financial services powerhouse, Bankers Trust Corp. After 10 months, at 26, he was made a vice president. As at Fitel, however, Bezos faced resistance to the technology he was developing.

By 1990, Bezos was tired of being a technologist at a non-technology company. But a headhunter urged him to consider one more: D.E. Shaw.

It had an allure as one of the most technically advanced financial shops in the world. The founder, David Shaw, had a PhD in computer science from Stanford; he was interested in both technology and finance, and was an expert in devising new trading strategies based on complex mathematical formulas.

Shaw was a 'true genius', Bezos says, a person unusually adept at using both sides of the brain, seeing big pictures and small patterns. Bezos learned many business practices from Shaw and later incorporated them at Amazon. Even hiring at Amazon was done along the lines of Shaw's philosophy, 'We don't always recruit for specific positions. We're happy to warehouse a truly gifted individual on the assumption that they may someday make us money.'

After two years, Bezos was named a senior vice president, becoming, at 28, the youngest of four at Shaw. He spent much of his time exploring new business opportunities for the firm. Bezos spent many nights in a sleeping bag he kept rolled up in the back of his thirty-ninth-floor office.

In early 1994, Bezos began working directly with Shaw to investigate business opportunities online. After decades on the esoteric fringes, the Internet was becoming mainstream with the advent of the World Wide Web. Bezos had first used the Internet in 1985, in a Princeton astrophysics class, but he never thought about its commercial possibilities until the spring of 1994, while working for Shaw.

Bezos and Shaw met for a few hours each week to brainstorm ideas; Bezos would then go off on his own and research them. He enumerated twenty products that could be sold online, among them software, trading services, compact discs and, somewhere down on his list, books.

Of these, the books kept rising. They could be easily sampled online. There were about 3 million books in print at the time, 10 times the number of CDs. The Internet's search capabilities made it easy to browse by author, title, publisher and keyword, an arduous process in a physical bookstore.

Bezos's research coincided with another realization: he was ready to start his own business. He had contemplated possibilities for years, increasingly as he approached 30. At that time, he was the company's youngest-ever vice president and became senior vice president two years later.

Meanwhile, several media reports during the early 1990s raised questions about the hype about the Internet. Even as some daring individuals were working on launching their online projects, the reports raised questions about their survival.

Bezos, however, was optimistic about the future of the Internet. 'I came across the fact that Web usage was growing at 2,300 per cent per year. I'd never seen or heard of anything that grew that fast, and the idea of building an online bookstore with millions of titles — something that simply couldn't exist in the physical world — was very exciting to me,' Jeff told the audience in his 2010 Princeton address.

At that time, the US Supreme Court had passed a ruling by which it exempted mail order businesses from sales tax in states where the companies did not have any brick and mortar outlets. Bezos did some research and settled for books as his first online offering.

During that time, he had been married for a year. 'Mackenzie had married a stable, working Wall Street man who one day went and told her he wanted to quit his job and start an online book company. I even told her that probably it wouldn't work since most start-ups don't, and I wasn't sure what would happen after that. Her reaction, even before she asked me what the Internet is, was let's do it,' Bezos said in an interview.

But not everyone was on board.

'What do you mean, you are going to sell books over the Internet?

That was Mike Bezos's first reaction when his son called to tell his parents about his plans to launch Amazon in the mid 90s.

Brad Stone describes this situation in his 2013 book, *The Everything Store*. According to Stone, Mike and Jacklyn had been in Colombia for three years, where Mike was working as a petroleum engineer for Exxon.

During that time, they had used a now-defunct online service called Prodigy to keep in touch with family members, which meant that they weren't fearful of new technologies.

Mike Bezos told Stone that their hesitancy was more about Jeff Bezos leaving a cushy job on Wall Street to pursue something much riskier.

Stone writes that Jacklyn advised her son to work on his new venture on the side. Bezos reportedly told her, 'No, things are changing fast,' and, 'I need to move quickly.' It took some time for Bezos to convince his parents, but they finally came on board.

When Bezos told his boss at D.E. Shaw about the plan, they were walking through Central Park. They talked for two hours. Shaw told Bezos that even though it sounded like a 'really good idea', it would be even better for someone who didn't already have a good career. 'That logic made some sense to me, and he convinced me to think about it for 48 hours before making a final decision,' recalled Jeff Bezos. Shaw told Bezos that he could have a bright future at the firm but said that he understood his desire to start something of his own, something that Shaw himself had done when he left Morgan Stanley in 1988.

Bezos took forty-eight hours to make a final decision. He contemplated in what he calls a regret-minimization framework. 'Most regrets in life are of omissions, not commissions,' he says. He placed himself in a rocking chair at age eighty, asking what he would regret more: leaving a job that came with perks like a six-figure Christmas bonus, or missing out on the chance to shape the Internet.

Bezos gave Shaw his final answer. 'I decided I had to give it a shot. I didn't think I'd regret trying and failing. And I suspected I would always be haunted by a decision to not try at all. After much consideration, I took the less safe path to follow my passion, and I'm proud of that choice,' said Bezos in an interview.

He chose Seattle to start his venture. The two most important aspects of running a business and the reasons why he did so were: talent and taxes.

When it comes to technology companies in Seattle, as well as companies in general, Amazon reigns supreme. However, coming from a position on Wall Street, it came as a surprise that Jeff Bezos chose Seattle to headquarter his company.

However, it shouldn't be that surprising. When it comes to potential hires for business and engineering positions, Seattle has a plethora of talent. The city attracts talent from across the country. As Bezos said in an interview, he wanted to start his venture in Seattle as he wanted to tap technical talent from Microsoft, which is also based there.

The other reason was taxes. As one of the first online retailers, Amazon would be able to take advantage of a tax loophole. Merchants who do not possess a physical location in a state, whether it is a brick-and-mortar store or an office, do not have to collect sales tax.

Had Bezos decided on establishing his headquarters in a larger state like California or New York, he would have had to collect sales tax on any sales in that state.

Seattle was the perfect city to create the perfect online retailer because of their abundance in talent and a low population, granting Amazon the ability to avoid paying severe tax rates.

FROM CADABRA TO AMAZON

'Be stubborn on vision but flexible on details.' The world's first online bookstore, Amazon. com was founded in Jeff and Mackenzie Bezos's garage on 5 July 1994. Interestingly, the company's name wasn't Amazon initially. 'I wanted to call it "cadabra" as in from "abracadabra", the magician's favourite word. However, when I told my attorney about the name, he mispronounced it as "cadaver"! When I told my friends, they too pronounced it as "cadaver" and then I realized it was the wrong name,' Bezos recalled in a chat show with Mark.

Thereafter, he decided to call it 'Amazon' after one of the world's longest rivers in South America.

Talking about why he chose books as the first

product for the company, Bezos said that both he and Mackenzie were avid readers. During his search for good books, he found that at any given point in 1994, there were 3 million books in publication while the largest physical bookstore had only 150,000 books to sell. The gap between demand and supply was huge, and Bezos felt that an online bookstore could bridge this gap easily and this is exactly what he planned to do.

Once the project was clear, a business plan had to be formulated. Mackenzie and Jeff Bezos decided to go on a cross-country trip. The couple was planning to take their dog also on the trip, but Christina volunteered to keep him instead. 'It was very practical of Christina, otherwise there would have been a lot of hassles,' recalled Bezos during a talk show with Mark.

It was during the trip from New York to Seattle that Bezos wrote the business plan for Amazon.

Now, the Herculean task was to get investors to back the idea. Here, Bezos's parents chipped in. The couple invested $100,000 in Amazon in 1995, even though their son had warned them there was a 70 per cent chance that they'd never see that money again.

Mike Bezos said that even though they'd seen the

business plan, they didn't exactly understand it, but they 'were betting on Jeff'. That their belief in their son paid off was an added bonus. 'It couldn't happen to two nicer people,' Jeff Bezos acknowledged at the Vanity Fair New Establishment Summit. Today, Jacklyn and Mike Bezos are the founders, and the president and vice-president, of the Bezos Family Foundation. According to its website, the foundation focuses on improving education and life outcomes for children.

Apart from family, there were around twenty to twenty-two external investors who gave around $50,000 each, for a less than a 1 per cent stake in the company. In all, they got about a 20 per cent stake in Amazon. These investments happened between 1995 and 1996. Incidentally, Bezos even warned all of them that there was around a 70 per cent chance of the venture falling through and going bankrupt.

Amazon.com opened for business in a garage that was full of extension cords and a stove, three large computers and three engineers, the founder and his first two employees. Their first goal was to show that this new industry could be self-sustaining. Growth would be steady and methodical and funded by whatever profits the company could muster; other outside investments would come later.

That was the traditional retail model. But the plan changed almost as soon as Amazon opened for business, in July 1995. In Amazon's first week, it processed $12,438 worth of orders. To record the number of sales, a bell was installed in the garage, to ring every time a book was sold. However, within a week, the bell was removed as the sales figure went through the roof. Within a month, the company had sold books to people in all 50 states and this had been done without any advertising.

Internet commerce was becoming a big thing overnight.

The company had ten employees at that time, including sophomore engineers. 'We were packing books day in and day out. I remember once, after a particularly long stint on our hand and knees while packing books, I told my staff we should get knee pads. One of them remarked that we need packing tables instead of knee pads. I agreed and got tables. This doubled our efficiency and we started packing more books in the same amount of time,' Bezos told Mathias Dopfner in an interview.

In the initial days, Jeff Bezos would take the packages

to the post office himself in his car and also struck up friendships with the guys there. 'I thought maybe one day we would be able to afford a forklift,' Bezos said during an interview with American television journalist and former talk show host Charlie Rose in 2016. 'And it is very, it's very, very different today.'

Mackenzie put her literary career aside and did accounting for her husband's company in the first year. 'She wasn't ideally suited to be an accountant but did a pretty phenomenal job,' said Jeff.

Amazon soon outdid the market expectations. 'Within the first few days, I knew this was going to be huge,' Bezos said about the launch. 'It was obvious that we were onto something much bigger than we ever dared to hope,' he said. The online business allowed him to sell books that he did not have to personally buy and store somewhere. He could sell books that were kept in the warehouses of publishers and suppliers. This also helped save a lot of money.

For a brief period late in 1995, Amazon was slightly profitable, a milestone Bezos would renounce as 'unfortunate'. Profits meant stinting on marketing, advertising and infrastructure. Now, those three elements formed a tripod supporting Amazon's new corporate mantra: 'Get Big Fast.' Bezos knew that to survive, Amazon had to up its ante on two things: innovation and size.

Amazon finished 1996 with sales of $15.7 million, a jump of 3,000 per cent over 1995. Its losses were $6.2 million, compared with $303,000 in 1995. But by this time, investor trepidation about the Internet had succumbed to early-stage hysteria. 'I would give them pieces of paper with our weekly sales growth,' Bezos says, 'and they would say, "Where do we send the cheque?"'

Amazon wanted to use technology to change not only the delivery of products, but also the paradigm of shopping. Its engineers developed a 'collaborative filtering' software that would customize the shopping experience to each user's tastes.

Bezos sees this as a crucial achievement of his rise. He challenges any comparison between Amazon and established retailers such as Wal-Mart Stores Inc. No matter how huge they might seem, bricks-and-mortar superstores are intrinsically limited. 'You can subdivide the demographics of these stores into maybe 50 segments,' Bezos says. But Amazon caters to segments of one, each customer, several million of them.

'Jeff is launching this giant cruise missile in a general direction, but he doesn't know where it is going,' said Paul Saffo, director of Silicon Valley's Institute for the Future. 'He's inaugurated a business model of "Ready, Fire, Steer," not "Ready, Aim, Fire."'

In May 1997, Amazon went public and by the end of the year, the value of the shares had risen by 233 per cent.

The employees seemed very excited and Bezos sat them down to explain something. 'I told them that today the stocks are up by 100 per cent and so might feel that much smarter but what would happen when they fell? Would you all like to feel so bad?' The response to this was a resounding 'No'. The pep talk seemed to have an effect on the employees, who started concentrating on revving up business rather than focusing on the volatile stock market.

Meanwhile, in pursuance of his motto 'Get Big Fast', Jeff Bezos upscaled his business, for which he sought investors. Once again, as in the initial days of Amazon, he warned the investors not to expect any profit for the next four to five years, as he planned to reinvest all the surplus revenue into the business.

Bezos was named *Time*'s 'Person of the Year' for

1999, and one analyst dubbed him the author of 'one of the smartest business strategies in business history'. Hailed as an Internet pioneer, Bezos continued to take giant leaps in the virtual world even as the company did not make much profit at that time. In fact, as Bezos admitted in an interview later, in 2000 when the market crashed, Amazon shares fell to just $6. Once again, he convened a meeting of his employees. 'In the short run, the stock market is like a voting machine, while in the long run, it is like a weighing machine,' he told them and advised them not to get excited or perturbed based on the stock market's performance.

Even as the market was tumbling, Amazon's business was picking up. After studying the business trend, Bezos was assured that they were headed in the right direction and had nothing to worry about. Amazon surged ahead, with the online business booming even as other sectors spiralled down.

The conviction in his beliefs and focus on customers had paid off in the long run.

SCALING UP AND COMPETITION

'A brand for a company is like a reputation for a person. You earn reputation by trying to do hard things well.'

The competition, meanwhile, was heating up, with behemoth bookseller Barnes and Noble planning to start their own online bookstore in 1997. It was a battle of David versus Goliath. Although Amazon had a headstart of two years in the business and a team which had grown from 10 to 125 people with $60 million of annual sales, they were a mere patch on the 30,000 employees and $3 billion dollar annual sales of Barnes and Noble.

At that time, there were several media reports about the imminent failure of the fledgling company.

Jeff Bezos recalled one headline that particularly impacted him, 'Amazon.toast'. 'At that time, we were really scared. I called a meeting with all the 125 employees. The situation was quite bad and we were scared. In fact, parents, especially mothers, of most of my employees were calling up and asking whether they were doing okay. It was a scary time. I told my staff not be afraid of our competitors as they aren't going to pay the money. Stay focused on customers, 'cause it is they who make money,' Jeff told his employees and the rest, as they say, is history.

Amazon survived and how.

After books, the company started offering music and videos sometime in 1998. In fact, Bezos went a step ahead and asked customers what else they wanted to buy from an online retailer. 'I sent an email message out to the customer base, actually a thousand randomly selected customers, and I said, besides books, music and videos, what would you like to see us sell? And the list came back incredibly long,' explains Bezos.

'It was basically just whatever the person had on their mind right now,' recalls Bezos.

'One of the customers said, "I wish you sold windshield wipers because I need windshield wipers for my car." A light kind of went on in my head. You know, people — people will want to use this new fangled e-commerce way of shopping for everything,' Bezos tells Rose.

'People are very convenience-motivated,' says Bezos. 'So, that really kind of started the expansion into all categories, consumer electronics, apparel and so on.'

Expand he did. He invested in technology and also gradually started buying out potential competitors and complementary businesses over the years, making Amazon the leading online retailer all over the world.

After securing the top spot, Amazon began to focus on technology development. Amazon Kindle was introduced in 2007 as a lightweight device for reading electronic books. It was responsible for the creation of the e-book market in the US and abroad.

However, the journey was not without its ups and downs. There were mistakes on the way and the company faced criticism when it accidentally let its Kindle users access the book *1984*, which had a complicated history of copyright issues. The book, which was not in the public domain, was allowed to release in a few countries only. However, due to some technical glitch, Kindle users all over the world could access it, which was illegal. The company faced severe criticism and backlash, following which Bezos admitted that they sneakily accessed Kindle accounts and removed the book from the virtual libraries of users in countries where the book was facing copyright issues. 'It was like sneaking into your home and removing stuff,' he tells Dopfner.

However, when questioned, Bezos said he would continue to enter into new product categories and was not intimidated by lack of expertise. 'I am never disappointed when we're not good at something because I think, well think how good it's going to work when we are good at it,' Bezos says. 'And the apparel is like that. There is so much opportunity. Nobody really knows how to do a great job of offering apparel online yet. And we have tons of inventions and ideas and are working our way through that experimental list.'

As per some reports, Amazon is the largest online apparel seller in the world, outdoing the leader in the fashion and accessory departmental store segment, Macy's in the United States.

Today, you can buy almost everything from Amazon: from electronics to furniture and fashion among other things. The company has also made forays into technology, digital entertainment and cloud storage, and all these segments have only strengthened its position as a market leader in its sector.

FROM E-COMMERCE TO MEDIA

'The common question that gets asked in business is, "Why?" That's a good question, but an equally valid question is, "Why not?"' The next stop for Bezos was entertainment. It started with Amazon Studios and Amazon Web Services, to name two ventures. Prime, the e-commerce giant's popular two-day shipping membership, gives access to consumers to watch premium television shows. As per unconfirmed reports, Amazon Prime has 65 million members across the globe. 'We have developed Prime as the best of Amazon. Anyone who is a Prime member gets the best that there is,' remarked Bezos in an interview.

When questioned about how Prime helped Amazon,

Jeff Bezos said that when a person becomes a Prime member, they start buying more, simply to avail the benefits.

In addition, producing several hit shows, like the Julia Roberts starrer *Homecoming* and the Emmy-winning *Transparent*, in which a patriarch opts for a sex change operation, has led to more subscriptions. He also enjoys the creative freedom that the company gets by catering to a niche audience rather than to a vast TV audience. 'It allows one the freedom to tell stories that are narrower but incredibly powerful and well told,' he says.

Speaking about Amazon Web Services, Bezos says that they had hit the jackpot with it, as never before in the history of any business enterprise, did a pioneering venture get a seven-year time frame with no competitors. This gave them more than enough of a window of opportunity to launch and establish themselves in the market. 'We started the Web Services and there was no like-minded competition for seven years. No one took us seriously and by the time the competition came along, we were well on our way,' he said incredulously, during an interview with Rubenstein.

Usually, a pioneering company gets a two-year

head start, Bezos said, giving examples from his own life. When Amazon.com began selling books online, Barnes and Noble began their online venture two years later. Similarly, when Amazon launched Echo/Alexa in 2014, Google followed suit with Google Home in 2016. However, Amazon's Web Services got the 'best stroke of luck', in the words of the billionaire founder.

Apart from producing online shows, Bezos also bought *The Washington Post* in 2013 for $250 million. Bezos did not do any due diligence before buying *The Post* because he relied heavily on Don Graham, the 'most honourable person in the world' according to Bezos.

'I bought it because it's important,' says Bezos. 'I would never buy a financially upside down salty snack food company. You know, that doesn't make any sense to me. But *The Washington Post* is important. And so it makes sense for me to take something like that, and I also am optimistic. And I thought there were some ways to make it—I want it to be a self-sustaining, profitable enterprise,' he elaborates. 'And I think it can be done.'

'Our approach is very simple. It can go from being a local paper to a national and even a global publication. It is super expensive but it can be done in digital form,' outlines Jeff Bezos. And today, *The Washington Post* is making profit through digital avenues and the staff intake is also increasing, affirms Bezos.

He also bought Whole Foods in 2017. Bezos's empire now stretches far and wide, and in 2019 is valued at $1 trillion.

THE VISION

'I believe you have to be willing to be misunderstood if you're going to innovate.'

Throughout Bezos's professional and personal life, one thing has stood out—belief in himself. Hence, even when he was cautioned against his belief about the Internet boom, he merely smiled and proceeded to realize his vision.

The ability to sense the real potential of the Internet and see the way it would gradually become an inseparable part of households, despite the old guard advising him against his ventures, kept him going. During a TED talk, Bezos told the audience that his thought at that time was, 'We're very, very early,' as he believed that only the tip of the iceberg had been scratched, and there was much more in store in future.

It was this vision, coupled with the company's 'customer-centric' approach that has resulted in its stupendous success. As Jeff Bezos had famously told Rose, '[The] thing that connects everything that Amazon does is the number one — our number one conviction and idea and philosophy and principle which is customer obsession, as opposed to competitor obsession. And so, we are always focused on the customer, working backwards from the customer's needs, developing new skills internally so that we can satisfy what we perceive to be future customer needs.'

Another important business strategy is his 'willingness to think long-term'.

'We are very happy to invest in new initiatives that are very risky, for five to seven years, which most companies won't do,' Bezos said in an interview and added, 'it's the combination of the risk-taking and the long-term outlook that make Amazon, not unique, but special in a smaller crowd.'

'Being an inventor is very important. You can't skip steps. There are no shortcuts. Take one step at a time. It is easy to have ideas but very hard to turn them into success. To be an entrepreneur, you have to be stubborn on your vision but flexible on the details. As you go along pursuing your vision, you need to change the way you implement it,' he said in an interview.

Last but not the least, Bezos believes in plugging loopholes in the business and hence is obsessed about finding problems and solving them.

'Taking real pride in operational excellence, so just doing things well, finding defects and working backwards—that is all the incremental improvement that most successful companies are very good at... [Y] ou don't want to ever let defects flow downstream,' Bezos told Rose candidly. 'That is a key part of doing a good job in any business, in my opinion.'

And judging by his success, the opinions and vision seem to be worth emulating. 'Don't chase what is the hot passion of the day. This almost never works. You really need to be very clear of yourself. Project yourself to age 80 and then minimize the regrets that you don't want to have. I believe one should live for now while looking at the long-term perspective. There are a lot of paths to satisfaction and you need to find what works for you,' he told students during a TED talk.

THE LONG TERM

'If we think long term, we can accomplish things that we couldn't otherwise accomplish.'
After dominating online retail business, e-commerce, acquiring a newspaper and more, Amazon announced its decision to enter into healthcare business.

Jeff Bezos's other business interests include news organizations, technology, investment in Google, Uber, etc. In addition, Amazon has also acquired Whole Foods for a whopping $13.7 billion, as well as online shoe retailer Zappos and video streaming site Twitch. His venture capital investment company — Bezos Expeditions — has also invested in small start-up businesses. Bezos is also an investor in Twitter, Business Insider, Airbnb, to name a few.

As he expands his empire, Bezos just keeps getting richer. When Amazon's stock surged after news of the Amazon and Whole Foods deal hit, Bezos became a whopping $1.88 billion richer—that's $600 million more than what the top ten Whole Foods shareholders combined are making on their Whole Foods stock.

With Amazon hitting $1 trillion valuation in September 2018 on NASDAQ, the sky seems to be the only limit for Jeff Bezos. His 'customer-centric vision' seems to have not only hit all the right notes but also the bull's eye at the stock exchange.

After all, the man famously said, 'What we need to do is always lean into the future; when the world changes around you and when it changes against you— what used to be a tail wind is now a head wind—you have to lean into that and figure out what to do because complaining isn't a strategy.'

TRYING AND FAILING

'I didn't think I'd regret trying and failing.'
This quote aptly sums up Bezos's philosophy on failure, one that he has openly admitted from time to time across various platforms. Never one to hold back on innovation, Jeff Bezos has encouraged his team to think out of the box and anticipate what customers want next. Along the way, the company sometimes loses millions of dollars but when an innovation hits its mark, it more than makes up for the colossal losses.

As the man says, 'I have made billions of dollars of failures at Amazon.com. But these failures did not matter. Companies that don't experiment or take bets do not succeed. People want to know that they want to do something meaningful. We are working for the future. We have to be leaning into the future. We all have adversity in our lives. It's good as it teaches us to get back up after falling down.'

Here is a look at some of the prominent failures of Amazon.

The Amazon Fire smartphone cost the company $170 million in losses. The product launched in 2014, but flopped miserably and within a few months its price was slashed from $199 to 99 cents but to no avail. When asked about the loss by a newspaper, Bezos quipped, 'If you think that's a big failure, we're working on much bigger failures right now — and I am not kidding. Some of them are going to make the Fire Phone look like a tiny little blip.'

During the turn of the millennium in 1999, Amazon acquired a 50 per cent stake in Pets.com. Bezos invested around $50 million in the company, but the business went kaput in 2002. Later, Bezos also invested $60 million in Kozmo.com. The company that promised to deliver goods to consumers within an hour of ordering, folded up its business within a few years. In all, Bezos lost around $110 million in both these businesses.

'I've made billions of dollars of failures at Amazon.

com. Literally, billions of dollars in failures! You might remember Pets.com or Kozmo.com. It was like getting a root canal with no anesthesia. None of those things are fun. But they also don't matter,' Bezos said in an interview.

Bezos's travel reservation service, Amazon Destinations was launched with much fanfare in April 2015, but within six months the company shut down. The focus was on booking holidays to short, local tourist destinations but there were hardly any takers. When asked about the failure of his projects, Bezos in his commencement address to Princeton's class of 2010 said, 'I didn't think I'd regret trying and failing...and I suspected I would always be haunted by a decision to not try at all.'

Kindle users unknowingly bought two books of George Orwell—*1984* and *Animal Farm*—from an unauthorized seller. When Amazon came to know about the goof-up, they immediately 'snooped' into the users' accounts and deleted the books. They faced a lot of backlash for it, and Bezos was quick to admit his company's mistake and issue a public apology. 'Our solution to the problem was stupid, thoughtless and painfully out of line with our principles,' he said, adding, 'it is wholly self-inflicted, and we deserve the criticism we've received. We will use the scar tissue from this painful mistake to help make better decisions going forward, ones that match our mission.' He even admitted that such mistakes did happen in larger organizations as opposed to smaller ones, since there were so many people involved in the process that a mistake on the part of even one could result in a goof-up like this.

Amazon Wallet was an e-place where consumers could store and organize gift cards and store loyalty cards. Launched in July 2014, Amazon Wallet folded up within six months. Bezos once again didn't seem to be perturbed, rather he told the shareholders via a letter in 2015: 'One area where I think we are especially distinctive is failure. I believe we are the best place in the world to fail (we have plenty of practice!), and failure and invention are inseparable twins.'

'Marketplace's early days were not easy,' Bezos told shareholders in his annual letter in 2014. 'First, we launched Amazon Auctions. I think seven people came, if you count my parents and siblings. Auctions transformed into zShops, which was basically a fixed price version of Auctions. Again, no customers.' Taking their cue from these two ventures, the company started its own marketplace platform and, in 2017, more than half the items sold on Amazon were from third-party sellers.

In 2011, Amazon launched its TestDrive feature that allowed users to test and use an app before deciding to buy it. However, within four years, the project closed down as people preferred to use free apps rather than buying one. Bezos's drive for experimentation and failure remained unfazed. 'We will continue to measure our programs and the effectiveness of our investments analytically, to jettison those that do not provide acceptable returns, and to step up our investment in those that work best. We will continue to learn from both our successes and our failures.'

Other notable Amazon failures include Askville.com, an information sharing site, My Habit, a fashion flash sale site and Amazon WebPay, a desktop-based online payment service.

The first to admit his business isn't perfect, Bezos's forthcoming attitude is refreshingly honest. Instead of trying to sweep failures under the rug or pretend they didn't happen, he faces challenges head-on. 'Very rarely are you going to regret something that you did that failed and didn't work or whatever,' he said in a 2018 interview with Mathias Dopfner, CEO of Business Insider's parent company Axel Springer. 'And I think that, when you think about the things that you will regret when you're 80, they're almost always the things that you did not do. They're acts of omission.'

When questioned about the criticism he faced because of faulty projects or mistakes like the one on Kindle, he replied, 'We've had critics be right before, and we changed. We have made mistakes. And you know, I can go through a long list.'

Incidentally, he also recently became the man who lost the maximum amount of money in a single day when the market crashed in November 2018. Jeff Bezos lost a whopping $19 billion in a single day as he took the mantle from Facebook founder Mark Zuckerberg who had also lost several billions when the markets had crashed earlier.

However, it made little difference to the man who seemed to take it all in his stride. In fact, sensing more future probabilities in the upcoming markets, Bezos has pushed for more investment in India where he sees a huge potential for Amazon's growth. It is one of his most profitable markets, where, like the Internet, its usage is growing by leaps and bounds. Although there is stiff competition from the existing online e-retailers Flipkart, Snapdeal, Alibaba and even online grocery sites, the e-commerce giant seems to be upping its ante to take on all of them.

Another thing that has changed vastly since the company's fledgling days is its aggressive advertising. Initially, Bezos relied on word of mouth, but as the company expanded, he realized the importance of advertising. As a result, most newspapers have front page advertisements of flash sales or festive sales being offered by the company, along with a push for digital and television advertising. Amazon Prime is also being leveraged for the same, with the company tying up with telecom service providers to provide free membership if an individual opts for a certain plan above a decided range. This even includes a tie-up with national telecom providers, in addition to private players.

When questioned about the change in strategy, Bezos replied that it was a necessary step to give the customer as much as possible with the smallest investment. When people realize that they can get much more with a simple subscription plan at a nominal price, then they go for it. In turn, of course, it helps the business, as the customer purchases more and more to get more value for their money. That Bezos has hit the mark with his strategy, is more than evident.

THAT X FACTOR

'The thing that motivates me is a very common form of motivation. And that is, with other folks counting on me, it's so easy to be motivated.'

In his many inspirational speeches, one thing that commonly stands out is Jeff's passion for his work and his ability to treat every day at Amazon as his first day. 'I don't want the enthusiasm to wane. As an enterprise grows, the number of employees also grows. Gradually, direct customer contact between the upper management and them starts decreasing. It is the lower staff that manages customers directly. A policy of treating every day as "day one" proves helpful, as everyone adopts a fresh approach,' said

Bezos in an interview with Ross.

Bezos's leadership role too has evolved from 1995 to today. Earlier, he would deliver the goods to the post office directly, and now of course there are several hundred employees and courier services to do that. But one thing has never changed — Bezos's involvement in his business. 'Although day-to-day management of the business has now shifted to the staff, my involvement is at the key policy level, and of course, if there is anything major, then I am completely involved in it,' he told Ross.

But one thing is for sure, Bezos surely misses his work. During a television interview, he confessed that the family had gone for a short vacation to Norway, which was planned by Mackenzie, and enjoyed it. However, he started missing work by the end of the week-long holiday. 'I couldn't wait to get back,' he said with his trademark laughter. 'When you love your work, which is also your passion, then you start enjoying it. And this is exactly how it is with me.'

And as with any success story, Jeff Bezos believes that there are no shortcuts to success. Working step by step is the only way forward, provided one is doing it with 'passion and ferocity'. '[At Amazon] we don't even take a position on whether our way is the right way,' he says, 'We just claim it's our way.'

A self-confessed 'goofy' guy, Jeff Bezos for all his billions of moolah, can be seen moving around at Amazon headquarters in casual khakis and a cotton shirt. Even in 1999, when *Time* magazine named him 'Person of the Year', he would walk around the office in casual wear, eagerly showing his ID card at every security clearance. Anyone entering the office at that time could have taken him for one of the staff members, but for the large picture situated in the foyer.

Today, a much more chic and slightly beefed up Bezos presents a different picture though. But his trademark laughter and enthusiasm remain the same. 'I am a very good audience,' he had told Dopfner in an interview. And the person who makes him laugh the most is his sibling Mark. 'I am laughing most of the time when I am with him, as he cracks the most funniest of jokes or anecdotes that I enjoy over beer,' he said, while smiling at his sibling during an informal talk show. As for Mark, he introduces himself as the 'Bezos with the lower bank balance', to which the brothers grin and the audience joins in the laughter.

The world has become Jeff Bezos's stage and he

now seems to be enjoying every moment of it, with his trademark guffaw hiding his sharp intellect and childlike enthusiasm for innovation.

LOOKING AHEAD—BLUE ORIGIN

'You don't choose your passions. Your passions choose you.'

Lying on his stomach on the living room carpet, watching Neil Armstrong become the first man to land on the moon, young Jeff Bezos did not blink even once as his eyes remained glued to the television set.

As Armstrong planted the American flag on the moon's surface, the entire family cheered and five-year-old Jeff beamed, for he had found his calling—space travel. After the mentorship of Pop Gise and a diet of *Star Trek*, Bezos's fixation with outer space grew. He had always been taken with far-off exploration and magical kingdoms: he had visited Disney World seven times!

'This is a childhood dream,' Bezos tells Ross. 'I fell in love with the idea of space and space exploration and space travel when I was five years old. I watched Neil Armstrong step onto the moon. You don't choose your passions, your passions choose you. So I am infected with this idea. I couldn't ever stop thinking about space. I have been thinking about it ever since then.'

In high school, young Jeff was valedictorian of his class and, in his speech, the entire focus was on space. The parting line was: 'Space, the final frontier—meet me there.'

Bezos believes that space travel is the future and space colonization would help save theEarth in the long run. Today, his obsession with space has taken the form of Blue Origin LLC, a multi-billion dollar project to find an alternate habitable planet for human beings and also to make space travel affordable. The company's name refers to the Earth, a blue planet, as the point of origin. Its headquarters is in Kent, Washington, while other offices are located in Texas, Florida and Alabama.

Founded in 2000, the company is developing technologies to make space travel cheaper and accessible for the general public. Blue Origin's motto is 'Gradatim

Ferociter', Latin for 'Step by Step, Ferociously'. In addition to developing several technologies, the company is also working on rocket-powered vertical take-off and vertical landing (VTVL) vehicles for access to space.

And this pet project of the Amazon honcho comes at a huge cost. By 2014, Bezos had invested $500 million of his own money into the project. In 2017, he said that he would invest around $1 billion annually into Blue Origin. The ultimate goal of the company is to send people to space on New Shepherd, its suborbital rocket. The first manned flight is expected to be launched by April 2019.

'Basically, what I am doing right now is taking my Amazon winnings and investing them. Every time you see me sell stock on Amazon, it's (to) send more money to the Blue Origin team,' Bezos tells Ross. On a chat show with Mark, he said that his long-term vision was to colonize space, with the aim of creating a place where trillions of people could live and work. 'Earth is a jewel in our Solar System and I want to preserve it. The only way forward is to ease the burden on resources and that is only possible if people start living on another planet. So, we can either go out into space or switch over to our civilization in stasis,' he said.

And the one word that Bezos doesn't like is 'stasis'. He calls it a waste of time, living in a state of limbo rather than taking any action. 'You might be out of a job, but rather than sitting and fretting about it, if you take some steps like forwarding your resume or meeting people about employment opportunities, then you feel much better rather than simply doing nothing,' he told Rose.

With Blue Origin, he is doing just that by taking his space programme ahead in a logical manner.

The first step in this direction is making space travel affordable. At present, it is very expensive, since a booster rocket is discarded every time it is shot into space. He wants to start a shuttle service that would spare companies the necessity of having to discard the booster rocket.

Conceding it to be a very long-term plan, Bezos said that his ultimate long-term objective of colonizing space is almost a several hundred year project. But in the short run, he aims to make space travel affordable. Incidentally, the short term objective also spreads across several decades.

'I meet many people who say they would like

to live on Mars. I tell them, do me a favour and try living in Antarctica or on the top of Mount Everest for a month, as they are a garden of paradise compared to Mars,' remarked Jeff jokingly in an interview, adding that it was important to make the environment human-friendly before colonizing it, and all this would take several hundred years.

In addition to making space travel affordable, Bezos is enthusiastic about building the infrastructure for the next generation of space entrepreneurs.

While normally people have eight-to-nine-year-long plans, Jeff Bezos's plan for his pet project is several hundred years. When questioned by Mark, this is what he had to say, 'Long-term thinking is a lever to make you do things.' And his ultimate objective is to have someone living on another planet be able to make inventions as easily as they do now on the Earth.

'[I]f I'm 80 years old, looking back on my life and the one thing I have done is make it so that there is this gigantic entrepreneurial explosion in space for the next generation,' says Bezos, 'I will be a happy, happy man.'

It was an icing on the cake when Bezos won the first Buzz Aldrin Space Innovation Award, which was instituted by the famous Apollo 11 moonwalker. Aldrin had gone with Neil Armstrong to the moon and was the second man to step on it. Aldrin even visited the Blue Origin office, with a wonder-struck Jeff Bezos showing off the innovations and experiments of his team. Lauding the billionaire for his initiative, Aldrin in a Facebook post said, 'I think of Jeff Bezos as a passionate patron of helping to shape the future of America's space program.'

A self-confessed *Star Trek* fan, Bezos had a cameo as an alien in the 2016 film *Star Trek Beyond*. He also appeared in an episode of *The Simpsons* in 2008, with fellow billionaires Mark Cuban and Mr Burns.

Meanwhile, another one of Bezos's long-term objectives is building a 10,000-year-old clock. The project is called 'The Clock Of The Long Now'. Sitting under a mountain in Texas, the clock is still under construction, and would tick once in 100 years and the gong would sound every 1,000 years! Bezos donated a piece of land in Texas and $42 million for this project. The objective is to leave something for posterity.

'We would all be gone by then, but someone somewhere will discover the clock and this is how discoveries are made and history unfolded,' he told the audience at a talk show.

MANAGING AMAZON/
HEAVYWEIGHT CHAMPION

'We've had three big ideas at Amazon that we've stuck with for eighteen years, and they're the reason we're successful: Put the customer first. Invent. And be patient.'

The core philosophy of the online behemoth that its boss has been following right from the first day, is: Customer obsession compared to competitor obsession.

With the company valuation hitting the trillion dollar mark in 2018, the one thing that has not changed ever since it was founded is obsessive customer obsession. Jeff Bezos never fails to underscore this fact. And it is this larger vision within which he has three other core values that every Amazon employee is expected to follow: eagerness to invent, long-term thinking and operational excellence.

'Customers will always want the following things: low price, quick delivery, more variety and convenience. If you are able to give them these, then they will be happy and well...you can do the maths yourself,' he said at a talk show.

One of his favourite quotes underscoring Amazon's core value is: 'The best customer service is if the customer doesn't need to call you, doesn't need to talk to you. It just works.'

However, when a customer emails complaints to Bezos, he forwards it to the concerned employee with a '?' in the subject line. Once the complaint has been resolved, the concerned employee replies to Bezos saying how it was resolved and that the case is closed.

Bezos also buys products from Amazon and one cannot help but wonder if the top boss too receives a wrong or damaged product. When asked, he shrugs and nods. So, does the concerned department immediately get a rap on the knuckles from him? 'No, I call up the concerned person and tell him/her about the problem, asking them to sort it out and also ensure that it doesn't happen with our customers. However, this is all part and parcel of the business,' he quips during an interview with Rubenstein.

To draw more customers, the company introduced Amazon Prime. The idea incidentally came from a junior software engineer at a meeting. He suggested an 'all you can eat buffet kind of shipping deal for Amazon customers' and after the logistics were worked out, Prime was implemented. It wasn't profitable initially, but relying on the logistics, Bezos and his team knew that they would hit the jackpot once they reached a certain volume of sales. It has been an upward ride since. 'Once people take the Prime subscription, then they want to get the best value for their money. Hence, more shopping and well...more revenue,' he tells Rubenstein.

So how does Bezos make such decisions that can either leave the company several million dollars short (as it had happened when several projects tanked) or even rake in the moolah (if it hits the bulls eye)? He tells Rubenstein, 'All my decisions are based on heart, intuition, guts, instinct and not analysis. Even when I wanted to start Amazon, I followed my heart. It was the same with Blue Origin.' As for failures, they don't bog him down. He seems to have mastered the art of failure and believes that failure and invention are inseparable twins.

It will not be wrong to state that Bezos's thinking is an integral part of the culture at Amazon. He summed up his philosophy in the company's recent yearly shareholder letter: 'I believe we are the best place in the world to fail (we have plenty of practice!).'

But here is the punch line: One project that hits the jackpot makes up for the millions of dollars of failures! And Amazon has had its share of successes that have sent its stock soaring by up to 70 per cent in 2018, making Jeff Bezos the richest man on the planet, replacing Microsoft's Bill Gates at the top spot of Forbes' annual list. Gates would have touched Bezos's $150 billion mark, but he has donated a major part of his earnings and shares to the Bill and Melinda Gates Foundation that is involved with several philanthropic causes.

When Rubenstein asked how it felt to be the richest man on earth, Bezos quipped, 'I was happy being at the number two position. There was nothing wrong with it.'

So how do these soaring stock prices make him feel? Bezos says that he would often sit down with the staff, even during the early days, when the stock price went up by 30 per cent and tell them not to feel '30 per cent smarter, because when it fell by 30 per cent, then no one would want to feel that much dumber.' He advises employees, 'In the short term, the market is a voting machine. In the longer term, it is a weighing machine. We want to be weighed, not voted upon.'

The rule applies even today.

Recalling the days when the Internet bubble was at its peak in the late 1990s before it burst, Amazon shares had gone up to $113 per share, but within a year, when the bubble burst, each went down to $6. The market was down and most Internet companies at that time downed their shutters. For Bezos, it was a hard time as well. However, he closely studied the internal business matrix of Amazon and found that while stock prices were falling, business was going up. 'Yes, it was difficult to get funding at that time, but we had enough money to sustain ourselves. I just waited patiently and bid my time, since the business was showing an upward trend and the rest, as they say, is history,' he tells Rubenstein.

One of the reasons for this is also the billionaire's belief of treating everyday at Amazon as 'day one'. He does not want the entrepreneurial spirit and nimbleness to die, which he believes usually happens in a large scale enterprise, hence the philosophy.

Meanwhile, his increasing wealth and influence have also drawn criticism and even the wrath of the powers that be. As per reports, American President Donald Trump has, in his tweets, often criticised how Amazon is hurting small retailers and also taking away jobs.

When questioned about the accusations, Bezos told Rubenstein that he was open for review as any large organization should be, since there is nothing to hide.

President Trump has also labelled the Bezos-owned *The Washington Post* as 'phony and dishonest', revoking the credentials of some of its journalists for 'inaccurate coverage and reporting of the record-setting Trump campaign'.

In fact, other than *The Washington Post*, Trump's love-hate relationship with the media is a known fact. In November 2018, during a press conference at the White House, President Trump and CNN reporter Jim Acosta got into a tiff over a question regarding the US administration's move to stop Mexican refugees entering

America. With Acosta questioning the President about the decision to stop them from entering the country, Trump tried to defend and when questioned further, told the reporter to sit down. Even as Acosta continued with his questioning, a White House intern tried to take away his microphone and when he persisted, Trump made some disparaging remarks about his integrity. Later, the White House cancelled his admit pass to the White House.

The move sparked widespread criticism, with even Trump's favoured *Fox News* channel coming out in support of Acosta.

When Rubenstein questioned him about the love-hate relationship between the administration and media, Bezos urged the powers that be not to 'slander media by calling them bad names,' saying, 'It's dangerous to demonize media.'

Meanwhile, the fact remains that Bezos's business moves affect the stock market. As an analyst said, the moment Bezos bought Whole Foods, the stock price of Amazon soared, but that of other companies in the same segment plummeted. Many even label him as a 'monopolist' saying that his business moves are bad for a healthy economy, since competition is being systematically wiped out. The billionaire, though, waves away these voices of dissent with a laugh.

However, as Jeff Bezos's business grew, he faced flak for not being involved in social causes. One of the surveys placed him last on a list of philanthropic billionaires, even as Bill and Melinda Gates continued to raise the bar with their foundation. As time passed, Bezos sought ideas from his customers on philanthropic issues that they wanted him to take. At one point, he received a staggering 47,000 suggestions, on email, by post and also on social media that his staff sorted into buckets and kept in his office. Two issues that struck a chord with him were education and homeless people.

To this effect, he started a foundation and invested $2 billion in it. The foundation lays emphasis on early education, as Bezos was also a Montessori student. He believes that helping a two-, three- or four-year-old child from a low-income group would give them a leg up and they will not fall behind subsequently. Bezos would be supervising a project along with his team, wherein they will identify genuine candidates and fund their pre-school education, to put them at par with children from middle-class and upper-middle-class backgrounds, as they seek admission to Montessori school. His mother also heads a foundation founded by Bezos, focusing on education.

For his achievements, Bezos has received several awards and degrees. Carnegie Mellon University awarded him an honorary doctorate in Science and Technology in 2008. U.S. News & World Report selected Bezos as one of America's best leaders. Bezos also received an Innovation Award from *The Economist* in 2011 for Amazon Kindle.

In 2012, *Fortune* named him 'Businessperson of the Year'. In the same year, he also received the Gold Medal from the National Retail Federation for serving the industry with distinction. In 2018, *Time* magazine named him among the 100 most influential people in the world, while *Harvard Business Review* ranked him the second best CEO in the world.

However, when asked if he liked being called the 'world's richest man', Bezos, with a twinkle in his eye and his customary laugh, said he would much prefer being called 'entrepreneur Jeff', 'inventor Jeff' or 'father Jeff'. Has 'entrepreneur Jeff' ever been denied a credit card transaction like lesser mortals? He chuckled and said 'Yes.' And what did he do then? 'Well, I take out another card and give it to the cashier,' he said, tongue in cheek.

SUCCESS MANTRAS

'Be willing to think long term.'
Some of the things that stand out across various interviews, talk shows and news articles by and of Jeff Bezos are the willingness to innovate and desire to minimize acts of omission from his life.

The most common question that Bezos encounters is how he manages to wear so many hats at once and maintain a work-life balance. The entrepreneur quips that it is not about work-life balance but about work-life harmony. 'I dislike the phrase work-life balance as by its very nature it implies one is trying to balance things at both ends of the spectrum,' he tells Mark.

Instead, he prefers using the phrase 'work-life harmony' and this is what he also teaches his staff, both at the entry level and at the senior management level. He says that it is very important to maintain harmony between one's personal and professional life and 'harmony' is a much more 'positive' word, when compared to work-life balance, which implies a constant state of flux.

And this harmony is something that the Amazon boss does with élan. For instance, he never schedules any early morning meetings, as he wants to have breakfast with Mackenzie and his children. Only after the children leave for school, does their doting father leave for work! In addition, he also likes to 'putter' during early morning, reading the newspaper and spending some quality time with himself.

During an interview with David Rubenstein recently, he said that meetings are scheduled at 10 a.m. and most high IQ level meetings are held before noon. After 5 p.m., Bezos prefers to take it easy. 'If anything comes up that would require a lot of brainstorming and is not urgent, then I tell my staff to schedule it for the 10 a.m. meeting the next day,' he says with a chuckle.

Having a multi-million empire to take care of, Jeff Bezos prefers to keep his mobile away when he is with his family. He likes interacting with everyone and 'be in the moment', he laughingly tells Mark, who remarks that even during their expeditions and cross-country trips or holidays he would hardly be on the phone because the idea is to enjoy the moment and experience it. 'I know that someone will eventually get in touch with me if it is something very important. And this usually happens when the news is not very good,' says Jeff, with a chuckle. 'The news then is usually about some medical emergency in the family or something that has gone drastically wrong in the business.'

This is something Bezos has in common with some other leading entrepreneurs and investors like Warren Buffet, who in an old interview had confessed that he did not even have a cell phone.

Ironically, a technology enthusiast and an owner of an e-commerce giant prefers family time without any tech contraption disturbing the quality time. He feels that real-world communication is more enriching, although he quickly adds that technology is the mainstay behind his lifestyle, as he has his managers and staff taking care of 'work' when he is not around. Does this help the Blue Origin chief to strike a work-life harmony? He nods emphatically and says, 'Absolutely'.

He is also not involved in the day-to-day operations

of the business as in the early years and leaves it to his top management to tackle daily issues. 'I, of course, get in the fire-fighting mode only when it is very urgent,' he tells Dopfner.

On any normal working day, Jeff Bezos is usually giving leadership and management lessons to his top executives and also to new entrants. Otherwise, he is at the Blue Origin office, seeing his long-term vision take shape.

A man with so many varied business and interests has to be good at multi-tasking, one guesses. Well, in Bezos's case, surprisingly this is not so! In fact, he likes to do one thing at a time. 'I am good at serial multi-tasking,' he tells Mark. In layman's terms, he likes to do one thing at a time. So, when he is reading mails, he doesn't want to simultaneously talk on the phone or do something else. When he finishes one task, he then proceeds to another. This habit is not something new. Even during his childhood years, he had the same thing going.

Jacklyn would often tell a story about her son in Montessori school. When a teacher would assign a task, the children would commence and when another task came along, they would change track. However, little

Jeff did not budge from his seat and would continue with the first task. The teacher would have to literally lift him along with the seat and take him to the next task station. Now, of course, no one can lift him, and Jeff Bezos continues with that same single-minded focus.

The Amazon honcho also likes to be among people with positive vibes. 'There are some people who enter the meeting hall and the atmosphere simply lifts up. You can feel the difference, while there are those who simply zap your energy as soon as they come in. The question that needs to be answered here is: Is your work place depriving you of energy or adding to it?' he asked students at a pep talk.

Answering his question, the billionaire entrepreneur said that positivity stemmed from liking what you did, if your work was your passion. And if this was the case, then you have hit the jackpot.

And he does try to make sure that the best minds work for him in the plush offices, with the amenities. He believes that it would lead to an increase in the work output if the workers are happy. The now iconic Spheres office of Amazon at Seattle with its spherical domes, housing a rainforest inside, with free office space, unlike the cubicle culture of the corporate world, gives a glimpse into what the philosophy here is all about—freedom to innovate and experiment, ultimately benefitting the customer. That the entire thing took seven years to build at a staggering $4 billion, underscores the man's philosophy.

And here is something else to ponder about: With Amazon's ever-expanding business, one would expect Jeff Bezos to be attending endless boardroom meetings. However, the reality is far from that. Bezos is famous for his 'two pizza rule' across the corporate spectrum. 'If a team cannot be fed with two pizzas, then it is too big,' he is often heard saying on several occasions.

He finds small teams to be more productive. As a former executive recalled, during a meeting at a retreat, when some senior staff suggested that employees should start communicating more with each other, Bezos called it a 'terrible idea'. He wanted individuality to prevail, rather than a herd mentality.

This is very much in sync with his philosophy of making fact-based decisions, as they overrule hierarchy. However, he is not averse to team decisions as well, because sometimes brilliant ideas come out of them, as he told Rubenstein.

LIFESTYLE AND PHILOSOPHY

'I think frugality drives innovations, just like other constraints do.'

For a man who made $104.7 million per day in 2017, as per *Business Insider* (India), frugality seems to be the opposite end of the spectrum. In 2018, when he became the richest man in history, the figure rose correspondingly. According to *Quartz* magazine, his net worth of $150 billion is enough to purchase the stock markets of several countries like Iran, Hungary, Nigeria, Luxembourg and Egypt.

However, in the early days of Amazon, Bezos had to be frugal. When the first few workers needed desks, Bezos found a cost-effective solution. He took a door and sawed at it to make a desktop, and added the four legs.

One of the early Amazon employees recalled how the door-to-desk culture came to being in the company. As orders were pouring in, employees needed desks to pack all the stuff and it was a pain to do so while bending on the floor. Bezos went around looking for desks on sale and found doors there as well, which were much cheaper than the desks. To save money and, of course, improvise, he decided to purchase a door and put some legs on it!

A token reminder of his frugal mindset still remains in the Amazon office, where Bezos's current desk is made out of a wooden door, according to a company spokesperson. Justifying his action, Bezos, in an interview with Bob Simon from CBS in 1999 said, 'It's a symbol of spending money on things that matter to customers and not spending money on things that don't.'

Hence, frugality remains one of the core principles of Amazon. The company gives the Door Desk Award to employees who come up with ideas that save money.

Bezos has also faced criticism from some quarters about the frugality in giving benefits to employees, but as he told Dopfner, 'I am open for public review. We have nearly 600,000 workers who are being given a salary and benefits as per the industry's norms. Some people criticize for the sake of it and well...I only take heed of constructive criticism.'

However, in October 2018, Amazon announced a hike in minimum wages to $15 per hour for its US and UK workers, a move that would benefit both its permanent and seasonal workers. The company had been facing flak for quite some time from the government, as well as from a certain section of employees for low wages, among other things.

On the personal front, even when Amazon had hit the $12 billion dollar mark after the company had gone public in 1997, Jeff Bezos had swapped his 1987 Chevy Blazer for only a modest upgrade—a Honda Accord. No one could have guessed then that it was a billionaire who was driving the car. When an acquaintance asked him about his choice of car, he replied, 'It's (Honda) a perfectly good car.' By 2013, he had upgraded to a slightly bigger Honda model.

Even in terms of appearance, Bezos would dress casually and was not seen in suits. His coat would hang in the closet at the company headquarters, together with those of other Amazon employees. He was often described as a 'nerdy' CEO with an astute business sense and leadership qualities.

As the company's fortunes began their meteoric rise, Jeff Bezos's persona and lifestyle also underwent a considerable change.

Until 1999, Bezos and his wife lived in a single-bedroom rented house in Seattle. Now, they own five houses across the US. According to *Business Insider*, Bezos is the twenty-fifth-largest landowner in the US today.

His houses include two adjacent properties in Beverly Hills, California: a four-bedroom home with a swimming pool worth £9.5 million and an £18 million, 28,000-square-foot mansion.

In 2012, he purchased four linked apartments worth a collective £12.5million in an Art Deco building on Central Park West, New York, according to Wealth-X.

His latest home is a 27,000-square-foot former Textile Museum in Washington, which he bought for $23 million and converted into a house. Bezos's neighbours include former US President Barack Obama and his family, and Ivanka Trump and her husband Jared Kushner.

Bezos also owns a $65 million private jet.

From a khaki and cotton shirt person, who would

casually don a blazer, today Jeff Bezos has had a makeover. From a lanky teenager to an athletic corporate professional, today the image that stands out and is one of the most shared ones, is that of a beefed-up Jeff Bezos, wearing sunglasses and a sleeveless jacket over a black T-shirt and jeans that even took his brother Mark by surprise. At a talk show, Mark compared the 'new avatar' of Bezos with the old one in which he was dressed in a Halloween costume during his skinny teenage years and said, 'This was the person I grew up with, so you can imagine my surprise when I got the new photo,' in response to which, Bezos laughed.

As for investing his money, Bezos certainly seems to have an eye for spotting a profitable venture. Bezos invested a reported $1 million in Google in the late 1990s, less than five years after he found Amazon.

Bezos has also invested in a vertical farming start-up called Plenty. The company grows crops on 20-foot-tall towers that are equipped with LED lights and don't need soil or sunlight. Plenty is on track to set up 300 vertical farms in China.

There are several other investments as well, and at the moment, Bezos seems to be laughing all the way to the bank with all the moolah, along with his shareholders. And what better place to edit the Amazon shareholders' letter than on his couch, accompanied by his children's giant stuffed panda. In his typical style, a bespectacled Bezos got a photo clicked in the comfy position as he was finalising the letters.

The man also loves taking selfies and being photographed in front of film posters. His latest fan boy moment was with Dwayne 'The Rock' Johnson. The entire family can be spotted going to see films. With Amazon Prime being one of the prominent revenue generators, his interest in the entertainment business comes as no surprise. In fact, Bezos is even seen with Hollywood stars at award shows in his chic avatar, with gorgeous Mackenzie by his side.

When not dabbling in business, Bezos can be found ensconced in his favourite couch with a book. This isn't surprising, as Amazon started off as an online bookstore. His favourite novel isthe Booker-Prize-winning *The Remains of the Day* by Kazuo Ishiguro. Later, it was made into a film starring Anthony Hopkins and Emma Thompson. The film received much critical acclaim and was even nominated for eight Academy Awards.

On weekends, one can find Jeff Bezos sporting his favourite Honey Badger T-shirt and lounging at the bar making cocktails, or sitting around the bonfire with the family sharing stories. During these times, Mark and Jeff Bezos have had many long-winding discussions, including business plans and the philosophy or logic behind their long-term goals.

Perhaps, it is this search for the esoteric or the desire to do something for posterity that motivates Jeff Bezos to keep going. After all, it was the natural inquisitiveness of the man that had him talking to small roadside shopkeepers selling *bhelpuri*, who particularly drew his interest, during his Kashi visit.

Walking through the vegetable market and capturing the vivid pictures with his camera, trying to speak a few Hindi words with the locals of one of the oldest cities of the world, where many foreigners and even Indians come, seeking the meaning of life and its ultimate purpose, just gives a glimpse into the man who wants to experience things first-hand, which also includes trying new kinds of foods, including the *sattvik* dishes of Varanasi.

The family left for Sarnath the next day, to visit the city where the Buddha had preached his first sermon to four students, after attaining enlightenment. As the Bezos family walked around the stupa and paid their respects in front of the idol of the Buddha, Bezos observed the peace on the faces of the Buddhist monks there.

As their vehicle made its way past the local shops and the Buddhist monastery, Jeff Bezos looked, once again, at the Sarnath stupa. One of the world's richest men observed the legacy that Prince Siddhartha had left for posterity, when he had left his kingdom to seek enlightenment and establish Buddhism, a religion that has spread to various countries today.

Every generation wants to leave something behind for posterity, but the Buddha gave us Buddhism, something that will last for eternity. For Jeff Bezos though, the eternity he wants to attain is through his Blue Origin project, when planets in outer space are colonised. Whether this dream will be realized or not is something that people can only know several hundred years later, today, as the man said: 'In the end, we are our choices.'

EPILOGUE

After 25 years together, Amazon founder Jeff Bezos and his wife MacKenzie decided to part ways. They announced their divorce through Twitter in January 2019, saying that they had decided to split 'after a long period of loving exploration and trial separation'. The message said that they plan to remain friends.

On 4 April 2019, the divorce settlement was announced by Bezos, making MacKenzie the third-richest woman in the world after L'Oreal heiress Françoise Bettencourt Meyers and Walmart's Alice Walton. It is likely to become the most expensive divorce settlement in history, with MacKenzie getting 4 per cent of Amazon's stock, which, valued at the company's then share price, was worth around $35 billion.

However, despite rumours about Jeff's relationship with former TV reporter Lauren Sanchez being cited as the reason behind the split, the respect and 'commitment for lifelong friendship' were apparent between the couple, as soon after the settlement MacKenzie tweeted, 'Grateful to have finished the process of dissolving my marriage with Jeff with support from each other and everyone who reached out to us in kindness.'

She further wrote, 'Happy to be giving him all of my interests in *The Washington Post* and Blue Origin, and 75 per cent of our Amazon stock, plus voting control of my shares, to support his continued contributions with the teams of these incredible companies. Excited about my own plans. Grateful for the past as I look forward to what comes next.'

Jeff Bezos is likely to continue his reign as the richest man in the world. According to *Forbes* magazine, he owned 12 per cent of the shares of Amazon, roughly valued at $110 billion as of July 2019.

BIBLIOGRAPHY

CNBC, https://www.cnbc.com/2018/09/13/jeff-bezosowning-washington-post-helps-support-americandemocracy.html, accessed on 18 September 2018

David Rubeinstein Show, https://www.youtube.com/watch?v=f3NBQcAqyu4, accessed on 1 October 2018

Forbes, https://www.forbes.com/sites/angelauyeung/2019/04/04/mackenzie-bezos-to-receive-more-than-35-billion-of-amazon-stock-will-be-worlds-third-richest-woman/#89bd76510013, accessed on 2 July 2019

Jeff and Mark Bezos Talk Show, https://www.youtube.com/watch?v=Hq89wYzOjfs, accessed in July 2018

Interview with Catherine Clifford for a website, https://www.cnbc.com/2018/05/07/why-jeff-bezos-

stillreads-the-emails-amazon-customers-send-him.
html, accessed on 20 July 2018

Interview with Charlie Rose, https://charlierose.com/
videos/17817, accessed on 27 July 2018

Interview with Mathias Dopfner, CEO of Business
Insider (Axel Springer https://www.youtube.com/
watch?v=SCpgKvZB_VQ, accessed on 19 June 2019

Kurt Schlosser from GeekWire, https://www.geekwire.
com/?s=jeff+bezos+by+Kurt+Schlosser, accessed in
2018

Report by Sally French, https://www.marketwatch.
com/story/its-not-just-amazon-and-wholefoods-
heres-jeff-bezos-enormous-empire-in-
onechart-2017-06-21, accessed on 30 September 2018

The Washington Post, https://www.businessinsider.
in/How-Amazon-CEO-Jeff-Bezos-reinvented-the-
Washington-Post-the-140-year-old-newspaper-
hebought-for-250-million/articleshow/52281125.
cms, accessed on 13 October 2018

Also in *The Making of the Greatest* Series

MARK ZUCKERBERG

by Abha Sharma

This is the inspiring story of Mark Zuckerberg, a young man who defied every bit of conventional wisdom to become the youngest self-made billionaire ever.

Even though controversy kept following Mark Elliot Zuckerberg from the time he created a rudimentary website for students of Harvard to rate each other, he went ahead undeterred to create the Facebook, the biggest social network in the world. Facebook has revolutionized the way people communicate, and it currently has more than two billion users worldwide. Its 'baby-faced CEO', who was depicted as a socially challenged, emotionless geek in the Oscar-winning movie, *The Social Network*, has demonstrated how to dream big and achieve it.

This biography explores the fascinating journey of Mark Zuckerberg and his many avatars—software programmer, fencing champion, Harvard dropout, founder, CEO, philanthropist, son, friend, boyfriend, husband and father.

BILL GATES

by Ajay Sethi

Encyclopaedia Britannica describes Bill Gates (born William Henry Gates III) as an 'American computer programmer, businessman and philanthropist' — and rightly so. However, the man and his achievements are so vast that even a big, fat encyclopaedia would not be enough to document his entire life.

In his teenage years, Gates acquired the reputation of being quite a hacker. At thirteen, he hacked his school computer and got himself into a class 'with a disproportionate number of interesting girls'. Then, at fifteen, he hacked the computer of a big corporation. He has even been arrested. His life took a dramatic turn in 1975 when he decided to drop out of Harvard. Soon after, he and Paul Allen co-founded Microsoft Corporation out of a garage in Albuquerque, New Mexico. By the end of the 1980s, Microsoft had become the largest software company in the world. A billionaire since 1986, Gates is currently the second richest man in the world, behind Amazon's Jeff Bezos.

This book is about a man who changed not only the way people live and work every day but also redefined the meaning of 'giving back to society' by pledging most of his wealth to charity.

JACK MA

by Abha Sharma

This is the incredible story of Jack Ma, who was branded as a failure but chose not to give up.

Jack Ma (born Ma Yun) studied at an ordinary institution in China and failed multiple times as a student, and yet he held on to self-belief and created the Alibaba Group, the largest e-commerce company in the world. He was rejected for more than thirty jobs, including that of a waiter, but a few years down the line, he was providing employment to millions of people. He first experienced the Internet at age thirty, but such was his business acumen that he built a company that wouldn't exist without the Internet. He learned English by talking to tourists, but he is one of the most admired public speakers in the language.

He says, 'If Jack Ma and his team can be successful, eighty per cent of the people [...] can be successful.' How did Jack Ma achieve all of this in the face of constant adversity?

Get an insight into the gruelling yet amazing work culture that he built at Alibaba. Jack Ma's story has that magical capability of invoking the best in people, to inspire them to persevere and keep moving ahead, and to make them think beyond self-interest.